The Ransom of Dond

SIOBHAN DOWD

The Ransom of Dond

illustrated by Pam Smy

David Fickling Books

Also by Siobhan Dowd:

For
Dave Shelton
and Ness Wood
with thanks for their help and support

and in memory of
Siobhan Dowd
who gifted us this beautiful story

'As we hauled in the creels, Dond came in from the sea, disguised as a black fog. He brought into our hearts the fear of dying and the desire for more. More fish, land, houses. More weapons, arguments, lies. In every man, woman, child, the lust for power was born. He decreed that Inniscaul would be washed away by a great storm if we did not pay his ransom . . .'

Darra read aloud the words of the sacred elders from where they were engraved on the standing stone at the tip of the headland. She'd recited them a thousand times before, but today she faltered at the last part:

'. . . *namely, the thirteenth child to a woman born. Any such child should be sacrificed to Dond at age thirteen and thirteen years of good fortune would follow. Otherwise Inniscaul would be no more.*'

The words were too close to the bone. Dond – the dark god of the underworld – had both chosen and cursed her. She was the dreadful ransom mentioned in the testament. She was

a thirteenth child and tomorrow she would turn thirteen. The fishers would gather at the cove below, and Cail would row her off to sea in a curragh. In full view of the villagers, she would leap overboard with a rock tied to her ankle. She would plunge to the depths of the ocean bed. She would die.

She could think of no worse birthday present.

In living memory, no woman in her village had given birth to a thirteenth child. The mothers knew too well what its fate would be. If they produced as many as twelve babies, they went to Olca, the mountain witch, who sold them a charm so that no more children would arrive.

Darra's mother, Meb, had had eleven children, all girls, who married among

the neighbouring families. When she
was expecting her twelfth, she
prayed for a son. The gods
listened – to a point.

As the old witch Olca reported, Bawn came first, white and wriggling. His little toes and fingers were perfect, his cries piercing and his hair red, the sign of a lucky life. But two minutes later the twin that nobody wanted or expected was born. She was wrinkled, dark and silent. Her mother pushed her away in horror. Olca named her Darra, meaning 'second'.

Cail, the village elder, had taken her in. He raised her in the great stone keep on the headland, apart from the other islanders, and taught her the elders' words: those engraved on the standing stone and others, passed down over generations.

She'd known from the day she learned to talk what destiny awaited her.

Cail had prepared her. He assured her
that her fate was not a bad one. Do not
be afraid, he often said. Drowning is a
pleasant death. A slow walk under the
water and then a sudden soaring up into
the light. You will be reborn as a fish,
a gull or a star, or maybe as all three.
You'll be free of human form and no
longer cursed. The great sky god, Lug,
will smile as you pass from this world
into Sidé.

Darra walked to the edge of the
headland. The sea below her was bright
and sparkling. Her black hair whipped
around her face. She didn't want to
be a fish. Or a gull. Or a star. She
wanted to go on being herself,
Darra. She wanted to live.

The curse of Dond unfurled inside
her. She became afraid to die. She sat
on the edge of the cliff and hugged her
belly, trying to press the fear back from
where it came. She prayed to the gods,
especially to Lug. But the sea crashed
against the rocks and the sun glided
west. She watched its rays lengthen.
A path of molten red shimmered
on the water. Her last day on
earth was nearly over.
She wept.

The sun sank in a purple flourish.

'Darra,' came a low voice nearby.

She leaped to her feet, brushing away her tears. A youth, a few paces away, crouched by the standing stone. Nobody from the village was allowed up on the headland. Had her tears brought forth a god?

'Who're you?' she gasped.

'I'm . . . I'm . . .' the youth blushed. If a god, he was a nervous one. He had freckles and rough hands, sharp green eyes with fair lashes, and a mop of orange hair.

'I know who you are!' Darra exclaimed, realization dawning. 'You're Bawn, aren't you?' Sometimes, from the headland, she had glimpsed Bawn's red hair out on the boats. He was said to be the luckiest of fisherboys. His creels came home full. She had often longed to meet him, but, because she was Dond's cursed ransom, she was forbidden to walk among the villagers in the cove below.

The lad nodded. 'Darra,' he said. 'I've sometimes seen you. Standing up here. Just a dark shadow on the head-land. I've often wondered what you were like – up close.'

'And I you,' said Darra. They looked at each other in silence. Then Bawn's lips twitched upwards into a half smile. Darra tried to smile back, but her lips went crooked and she found herself crying instead.

'To meet you now, just at the end,' she sobbed. He walked over and grasped her arm.

'Darra,' he murmured. 'My other half.'

'Oh, Bawn. I've missed you, even though I never knew you. It's lonely up here, with just Cail, the elder. He's always kind. But all I've ever wanted is a real home. A fireplace, music in the winter evenings, old folk, young folk – a mother, sisters – and a brother!'

'Here I am,' said Bawn. He wrapped his arms around her.

'I couldn't let tomorrow come without seeing you. But I didn't know how much pain I was bringing on myself.' He hugged her tight. 'If I could swap places with you I would. I never asked to be the first twin.'

'Nor I to be the second – I wish I'd never been born. What's our mother like?' asked Darra. 'She they call Meb? Will she be there tomorrow – to see me go?'

Bawn shook his head. 'I don't know. She's tangled in her head. People say that she carries twenty years over her age. She loves me, Darra; and pretends you don't exist. But, if you ask me, not a day passes that she doesn't think of you. Her love for me has gone wrong, somehow. She loves me too much. But nothing I do is right. She gives out if the creel isn't full, if I tear my clothes or eat too noisily. She wants me to be you, I sometimes think.'

'Supper time,' a voice called.

'Hide!' said Darra. 'That's Cail, come to fetch me into the keep. If he catches you, there'll be trouble. You've broken the Inniscaul rule coming here, you know.'

Bawn nodded. He squatted down behind the standing stone.

'I'll stay here,' he whispered. 'I'll
stay here tonight. By the testament.
Mam thinks I'm night fishing.
I'll watch out for you –
and pray to Lug.'

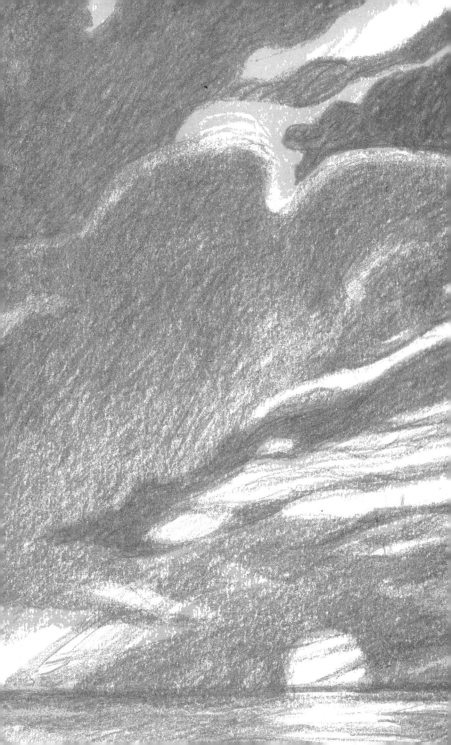

'I thought you were talking to someone,' said Cail over supper.

'I was. To the great sky god, Lug. He
came close to me tonight.' Darra found
she lied easily for someone who'd
never lied before. She crumbled her
barley bread into the steaming fish
soup and ladled a spoonful into her
mouth. She had trouble swallow-
ing, though, and replaced her
spoon.

'You are already passing,'
said Cail. 'To the Sidé –
the realm of fairies and
gods. You even look
a little transparent.'
He shook his
wise head.
'Darra,' he said.
'Drowning—'

'I know, I know. Drowning's easy. Easy-squeezy.' She giggled, then laughed until tears trawled down her cheeks.

Cail put a hand on her shoulder. 'Calm down,' he said. 'This is a solemn night.' He sighed. 'But I mustn't forget. You're young still.'

He led her up to her bedroom, a loft
with a skylight for a window.

'Sleep, dear Darra,' he said. 'Don't
worry. I'll be with you to the last. I'll
look after you, as I've always done.'

He patted her dark hair, and was
gone. She got into bed and shivered,
unwilling to blow out her solitary
candle. She stared at the flame and
thought of Bawn outside, keeping vigil
for her. The wax dripped. There was a
draft from the skylight, which made the
wick burn bright and fast. She yawned.
Her eyes grew heavy.

On the point of sleep, she heard the
candle flicker, then gust, and nearly
blow out. She started up in fright. The
flame sprang back to life with a loud
flutter, flapping and hissing, like canvas
on a high sea. She looked around, then

upwards at the ceiling. It wasn't the candle flapping at all, but a beautiful large blackbird, flying down through the skylight. Its blue-tinged wings were huge arcs, beating the air in her room so fiercely that her hair flew around her face. It landed on the bedpost by her head.

It stared at her. She stared at it. Its
head went off to one side. Its yellow
beak chirped.

'Lug,' she said. 'Lug or Dond.
Which is it?'

The bird looked as if it were
deciding: Lug or Dond, the god of the
sky or of the underworld – light or dark?

'Well, you're dark aren't you,' she
said. 'So you must be Dond.'

Then the blackbird spoke. Its beak
did not move, but she heard its words
in her head. They were calm words, but
Darra could not have said if the voice
was a man's or woman's. There was
music in the words like all the birdsong
of the island put together.

'No,' the bird said. 'I'm not Dond.'

'Lug, then?'

'Lug – if you say so.'

'Have you come to rescue me?'

'No. We can only rescue ourselves.'

'Well then: if not rescue me, perhaps help me find a way to escape my fate?'

'We must all fulfil our fate, Darra. But not even I know for sure what that fate is.'

'But I'm Dond's ransom. Surely you know that much?'

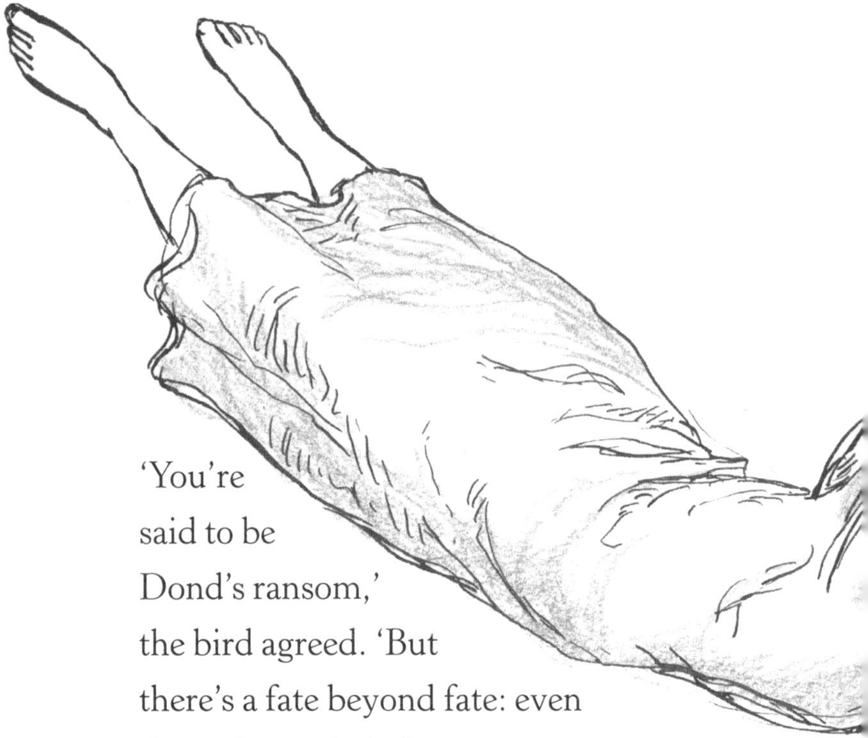

'You're
said to be
Dond's ransom,'
the bird agreed. 'But
there's a fate beyond fate: even
the gods get their fates wrong, sometimes. And then there's another matter.'

'What?'

'The small matter of truth.'

'Truth?'

The bird nodded. 'I have come to
show you it.' She looked into its sharp eye
and saw her face reflected there, her dark
brows frowning, her hair dishevelled. It
was as if she was drowning in her image.

She felt herself
sinking into the
glassy beadiness
of the eye, like
diving into a
cool, still pool of
water. The world
upended itself,
her stomach
somersaulted and
a great light flooded
through her. Instead of looking into
the eye, she was looking out of it. She
had entered the blackbird itself.
Before she could grasp what
had happened, he took off
from the bedpost and flew
up through the skylight. She
lurched around in the round
eye for lack of balance.

23

In seconds, she felt the chill night air. She saw a tangerine moon floating above the mountains, and out to sea, the summer dusk receding westwards.

The bird landed on the standing stone. Bawn was still there, curled up in a sheep's fleece, snoring.

'Darra,' he was muttering to himself drowsily. 'Darra.'

'It is a good thing I have two eyes, isn't it?' said the blackbird. He pecked Bawn gently on the neck.

Her brother started up. As he looked into the bird's eyes, he saw Darra looking out of one, and his own reflection in the other.

'I'm dreaming,' he said, pinching his forearm.

'No,' said the bird. 'This is beyond dreams.'

'Beyond dreams?' Bawn said.

'Beyond time. Beyond fate,' the bird answered.

'Beyond—' Bawn stopped and stared at Darra's reflection. 'What are you doing in there?' he said.

Darra giggled. 'Bawn,' she called, waving at him from the blackbird's eye. 'Don't be afraid. He's taking us to beyond our fates.'

The boy rubbed his sleepy eyes in disbelief, and, staring into the

bird's other eye, soon found himself
sinking into his reflection, as Darra
had done. Darra felt Bawn beside her,
warm and comforting. She linked
her arm through his.

'We're away,' said the bird. It took
off from the standing stone, and
wheeled over the headland. In the
failing light, they saw the candles of
the village in the cove below, and a
glimpse of the craggy oyster shape
that was Inniscaul Island. Beyond
that, across the water, was Eriu, the
great green landmass that few visited,
a brooding chain of mountains.

The bird swooped down. The view
vanished. All they could see was the
village below racing towards them.

Darra watched as the fishers' huts
drew near, simple structures of wood
and wicker. Dogs roamed. Spools of
smoke drifted from makeshift
chimneys. The blackbird landed on
a windowsill. The window was
nothing more than a rough hole.
In winter, a goatskin covered
it, but as it was a warm
night, the skin was
pegged aside.

'It's our home,' hissed Bawn.
'There's Mam!'

'Shush!' the bird commanded.

Darra peered in. By candlelight, she made out a woman by the fireplace. She had a shock of greying hair, large, sunken eyes and a shawl of tattered wool. She groaned to herself, rocking back and forth.

'Ah, Bawn,' she said.

And a few moments later, 'Ah, Darra.'

She stood up and walked around the hut. 'I'm going mad,' she cried. 'The thought of the two's of you. Curses to the two eggs inside of me where there should've been one!'

A knock came on the door opposite. Darra and Bawn's mother, Meb, froze. She crept to the door and opened it.

A gnarled woman, far older than
anyone Darra had ever seen, hobbled
in, bent double over a blackthorn stick.
Bottles of essences and bunches of herbs
rattled from a rope around
her bulging belly.

Her dress was a mix of fishing nets,
birds' feathers and badger skins. One
eye was gammied up with rheum, the
other shifted around the hut, a great
black mortar of a pupil, dilated, that
almost sucked you in if you stared at
it too long.

'Olca,' snapped Meb. 'Not you
again.'

'Regular as the moon,'
hissed the crone. 'Same as
every month.'

'Huh!'

'Payment day!'

'This is the last time,' said Meb.
She took a leather bag from a jug on

35

the mantelpiece and counted out five bright coins. 'My son Bawn is the best fisher in Inniscaul,' she said. 'Like his father before him. I make him fish night and day, and he little knows the reason I push him so hard.'

'He has you to thank, so.'

'Aye – but not you, with your black-mailing ways. If it weren't for you, neither Bawn nor his father would've had to fish so hard and long. My own dear husband might still be alive, not dead from a life of too much slog.'

She dropped the coins into Olca's hands.

'Didn't I deliver Bawn and his sister safely?'

'You did – you're a handy enough midwife, when a woman needs one. But you charge through the nose. And for thirteen years now, I've gone on paying you.'

The crone's hand stayed out, palm up, expecting more. 'Come now, Meb, my dear,' she croaked. 'Didn't I give you's a fine stout charm to kill the pain? And a lifetime of keeping whisht afterwards.'

There was complete silence in the hut. Then Meb shook the rest of the coins in the bag into Olca's hand.

'Take them,' she said. 'You horror. I hate you.'

The crone cackled and put the coins away somewhere in her ghastly folds. 'Hate's a great thing, altogether. The world won't turn without it.'

Meb shook her head. 'You, Dond, and the curse. Between you, you've made Inniscaul into a place of hate.'

'I seem to remember a little mite of
a baby, a tiny whimper, and a mother
taking one look, and saying – what was
it you said? "Take it away!" Wasn't that
hate itself?'

'I never meant it! Only I'd wanted a
boy so bad!'

'And you got one, didn't you?
A few minutes later?'

Meb paced the room, beating
her belly and moaning. Darra felt
Bawn stiffen.

'Never say that to me
again,' Meb moaned. 'Oh,
the lie I told that night! Oh,
my poor daughter. I'd love
her now, if she was safe
beside me. But Bawn
– the boy I'd always
wanted, a fair, fine lad

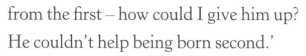

from the first – how could I give him up?
He couldn't help being born second.'

'No more than she could help being
born first.' The crone tapped her blackthorn stick on the floor.

'I feel like dancing a jig,' she
said. 'The joke you and
I've played on the village.
They'll drown a twelfth
child tomorrow, and keep the
thirteenth hale and healthy
among them – and what will
Dond, my master, do then?
He'll have a field day, with
the waves and pounding and
thundering. There's nothing
he likes better than a lashing
great storm.'

'Let Dond do his worst,'
said Meb. 'Bawn and I'll be long
gone. We'll be away in the curragh
and in Eriu before the day's out!'

'So you think!' the crone quipped,
waltzing around the room in glee.

Meb picked up a poker from the

fireplace. 'Get away, evil sprite!' she shrieked. 'I'll have no more dealings with you!' She brought the poker down hard on the crone's head, but no sooner had the blow fallen than the crone melted into yellow, choking smoke, smelling of onions and rotting fish. The fireplace sucked up the fumes and the last they heard of the crone was her maddening cackle going up the chimney. Meb dropped the poker and threw herself on the turf floor. She beat her fists and groaned. The blackbird flew off.

Darra curled up in the blackbird's eye, sobbing. Bawn was the thirteenth child, not herself. Her mother had wanted her gone the moment she was born. She felt Bawn shuddering uncontrollably beside her. All his

anguish, at least as great as hers,
rushed in on her. It was more than
she could bear. She fell out of
her senses.

～～෨ᴎᴑ～～

She woke the next morning, to find Cail smiling at her serenely.

'Darra,' he called. 'You've been dreaming – tossing all night.'

Darra crawled out from under the bedclothes. 'Was it a dream, then?'

'I don't know. Sometimes the gods come to us in dreams.'

Darra thought of the blackbird, her brother Bawn, the crone Olca and Meb, her mother.

'If it was a dream,' she said, 'it was the strangest ever.'

'When you draw near the Sidé,' said Cail, 'such dreams are common.'

'How would you know?' Darra snapped. 'You've never been close to death, have you? Not like me – soon I'll be dead, at the bottom of the sea, being eaten by fishes!'

Cail patted her head. 'The fishes won't eat you, dearest,' he said. 'You'll be with Lug by then.'

'Huh! Well, Lug, here I come.'

She got up and put on her dress of grey wool, and around her head, Cail tied a sky-blue ribbon.

'Dond claims you as ransom,' he said. 'But the blue shows that you are Lug's.'

He picked up his staff
of oak and led the way.
For the last time, Darra
left the keep that had
always been her
home.

They went over the brow of the headland, down the broken zigzag path to the village cove. Cail walked among the huts, shouting 'Dond's ransom!' People crept out one by one, and trailed after them, until they had drawn a huge crowd. He walked down to the shingle, by the sea's edge. A fine curragh was moored and waiting for them.

The villagers
hung back. Darra saw one
great fat man lick his chops like a dog.
She realized that they were happy to see
her die. Thirteen years of good fortune,
went the testament. Cail took from his
shoulder a hemp rope.

'Darra,' he said. 'You know what to do.'

Darra looked at the rocks at her feet
and picked a large black and white one,
dimpled in its middle.

'Here,' she said. In her head, a
strange buzz had started. She hardly
knew if she was afraid or about to faint.
As Cail tied the rope to her chosen rock,
she leaned against the boat's side. He
knotted the other end of the rope around
her ankle.

'Stop!'

The crowd gasped.

'This must stop,' a voice repeated.

Darra swallowed, trying to calm
herself. She looked around, and there
was Bawn. He approached her with the
light of Lug in his face. He was in fine
wool, like herself, and had tied a strip of
blue cloth around his head.

'I'm Dond's ransom,' he said. 'Not
her. I've come to tell the truth.'

The crowd gasped. Bawn stepped up to Cail. 'Great elder,' he said. 'You bring Darra to this moment, this day, thinking that you're doing right. But Lug came in the night, disguised as a blackbird. He showed me the truth:

a terrible truth. For thirteen years, my mother has lived a lie. I wasn't the first twin. When the witch Olca brought us into the world, Darra arrived first, not me. Darra was the twelfth child. I was – I am – the thirteenth.'

There was a general intake
of breath. Darra looked at Bawn.
Bawn looked at Darra.

'Isn't it so, Darra?' Bawn said.

Darra thought of Lug and Dond,
fate and time and truth. She thought of
curses, fortune and hate. She thought
of her brother, who did not
deserve to die.

'No,' she lied. She
stamped her foot. 'It's not
true. Bawn's trying to save me.
He's made it up! I am and
always have been the
thirteenth – drowning's
my fate.'

Cail stroked his
chin. 'Hmm,' he
muttered. 'I
wonder.'

The crowd shifted as
another latecomer arrived: Meb.
Tears streamed down her cheeks and
she flung herself at Darra.

'My baby!' she said. 'My jewel – oh, that I threw you away! And you've grown so grand a girl! Would you ever forgive me, in all the ages of the world?' She knelt at Darra's feet.

Darra found her hand on her mother's wiry grey hair. 'Forgive you?' she whispered.

Meb stood and kissed her. 'Please try to. My little stranger – my own girl. Can I have one last memento? A lock of your hair to cherish?' she said, producing a sharp little knife.

Before Darra could reply, Meb took a tress of Darra's hair and cut it off. She smelled it, stroked it. In the crowd there were mutterings of confusion and doubt.

Cail touched Meb on the shoulder. 'Meb,' he said. 'Your grief is understandable. But Bawn here tells a strange tale. That he was born second, not first; that he was thirteenth, not twelfth. That you lied.'

Meb looked at Bawn, astonished.

'I overheard you, Mam,' Bawn said.
'Last night. Talking to that wretch –
Olca. You've been paying her to keep
silent all these years. I'm sorry, Mam.
But Darra here could not help being
born first – or being a girl.'

'Overheard? How? You were out
night fishing, weren't you?'

Bawn shrugged. 'I lied,' he said. 'I
didn't go fishing. I went up—'

That fat man who'd been licking
his chops stepped forward. 'He admits
to lying – if about one thing, why not
another?'

Darra spoke up. 'He is lying – but
only because he wants to save me. Olca
delivered Bawn first, then me, as my
mother's always said. Isn't that right,
Mam?'

Meb looked at Darra. She looked

at Bawn. Then she turned to face the crowd.

'This is the truth,' she said. 'Darra and Bawn were born together, wrapped around each other! They are both the twelfth child.'

The fat man laughed his head off, and the crowd followed suit. Cail rapped the curragh's side with his staff.

'Shush! That's impossible, Meb. Twins are always born one after the other. Be frank and speak the truth, however painful. For only by the death of the true thirteenth child can Inniscaul escape Dond's storm.'

The fat man smacked his thigh and said, 'If they were born together, you could as well say they are both the thirteenth child. Let's kill them both and have done with it.'

'Kill them both! Kill them both! Kill them both!' the crowd chanted.

Darra got in the boat with her rock. Bawn tied another rock to his ankle and followed her into the boat.

'Get out,' he said to Darra.

'Get out yourself,' Darra replied.

'I'm the thirteenth.'

'You're not!'

'Am so!'

'Are not!'

'No!' screamed Meb. 'Not both!
I can't bear it!'

'Then tell us the
truth,' Cail said.

Meb shook her head. 'Lug!' she screamed. Her hands reached up to the sky and her mane of grey hair whipped up in a freshening wind. 'Lug!' she repeated. 'Have mercy on me this day! I've done plenty wrong in my life – but just this once, show me what's right!'

The clouds scudded across the sky. Waves cascaded on the beach. The villagers were silent.

'Show me!' she begged.

A bird swooped down, white in the sunshine, then dark as it drew close. It touched the crown of Meb's head, revealing itself as a blackbird, then flew off.

Meb did not move. 'The truth,' she whispered, 'is that Dond's curse is wrong. No child should die this way.'

'Rubbish,' the fat man roared. 'Now she's lying too.'

Grumbles and complaints,
whistles and sneers turned into
a low, hissing chant.
'Kill them both!
Kill them both!'

Meb stooped
down, picked a rock
and fastened it to her
ankle, using her
battered old shawl.

She stepped into the curragh and sat down between Darra and Bawn.

'We're a family,' she said. 'Where they go, I go too.'

Cail looked at the villagers. 'Three deaths – not one. Surely that is needless?'

'Let them get on with it!' said a thin woman with a pointed nose. 'And good riddance to them all, with their fancy ways and full creels! We want our thirteen years of good fortune!'

The whole village cheered. 'Sink 'em! Thirteen years! Good fortune! Get on with it!'

Meb shook her head. 'So much for neighbours,' she muttered. She took her two children by the hand.

'Come on, so,' she ordered Cail.

Cail sighed. He pushed the curragh off into the waters and sprang into its stern. He took the oars and rowed out towards the open sea. He stopped just beyond the cove, in full view of the villagers.

'My children,' he said. 'May Lug's light be with you. This is where you must jump.'

When it came to the point, Darra stood gripping her rock in the bobbing boat. She shut her eyes. She felt the air, the light, the faint warmth of sun. 'I'll do it,' she thought. 'On the count of three.'

She counted out loud. Bawn counted with her.

'One, two—'

On two, Meb leaped before them, feet first, her rock skimming after her. Darra saw her hair float for a second and vanish as the rock caused her to sink.

Bawn screamed, 'Mam!' and jumped
in after her. Darra hardly knew what
she did, but she was
over the side too,
gripping her rock
to her belly and
plummeting into the
waves. The cold slap
of water shocked
her eyes open.
She blinked.
Fear left her.
Underwater
was a quiet
and living
place.

Everything moved in slow motion. She drifted down. The light turned green-grey. An eel unfolded lazily and glided away. A shoal of fish scattered around her shoulders. Her ears were like drums, beating a last song. Drowning is a pleasant death, she heard Cail's voice echo. She held in her breath, reluctant to let the last air out, entranced by the silent kingdom.

Her feet hit the bottom. She was on the seabed. Bawn was standing next to her, his cheeks puffed out, his eyes as large as saucers.

Meb was there too, blue in the face, groping down the front of her dress, until Darra saw a gleam of a blade. A knife: the one she'd used to cut Darra's hair. Darra nearly lost the last of her breath in shock, thinking her mother

meant to stab her, but instead Meb
dived to her feet and cut the rope that
bound Darra to her rock. The sea
pushed her up like a cork stopper. Her
head broke the water and she coughed
and retched as new air flooded into her.
She bobbed on the water, staying afloat.

Ten seconds later, Bawn appeared,
his red head butting her elbow aside
like a nanny goat. She saw his cheeks
collapse and his face quivering white,
then red. Life that had nearly left him
returned.

'Mam!' he wailed. 'Mam!' He
sobbed and splashed his fists around.

'Oh, Mam!'

He pressed his cheek to Darra's.

'I saw her do it!' he said. 'She cut you
loose, then me. I tried to take the knife
from her. I clung to her middle, so that

the sea wouldn't throw me up, like it did you. But with her last strength, she kissed me and wriggled out of my grasp – like a slippery seal! And oh, her face, as Lug took her! She was smiling, Darra – smiling!'

He bawled out his grief and Darra joined him. They cried and trod water, and trod water and cried in the morning sun. They did not know what to do. They drifted further out to sea. Cail's curragh was nowhere in sight. Inniscaul lay a mile to the east. To the west, the great sea swelled to infinity.

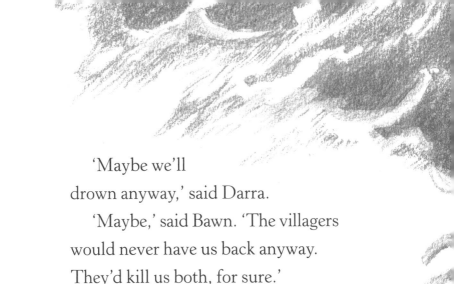

'Maybe we'll
drown anyway,' said Darra.

'Maybe,' said Bawn. 'The villagers
would never have us back anyway.
They'd kill us both, for sure.'

An unnerving blackness crept into
Darra, worse than any she'd ever
known. The sea heaved and crashed,
the waves grew larger. White horses rode
around them, charging like steeds in
battle. The sky went as dark as a puddle.

A crash rent the air in two.

'Dond's curse!' screamed Bawn.
Forked lightning hit the land to the east.
They bobbed and whimpered with fear,
holding hands. A great storm raged over
Inniscaul. It tramped like an angry giant
around the hills. One flash hit the
headland where Darra had lived with
Cail. Another crackled down to the
village cove.

Then it was over. It rumbled away
to the north, the sea settled and the sun
reappeared. Two rainbows formed over
the Inniscaul hills. As their colours grew
more vibrant, an empty curragh drifted
into Darra's line of sight. The storm
had loosened it from its mooring and
brought it out to sea.

'Bawn!' she said. 'The curragh! Look
at it! Lug has sent us this curragh. Let's
save ourselves.'

She swam to the curragh and rolled herself into it. Bawn followed her. He scooped out the water from the bottom and picked up the oars.

'Where to?'

'Anywhere – as long as it's away from Inniscaul!'

Bawn picked up the oars and rowed, but however hard he tried, a strong current pressed hard against him. Within minutes, it had driven them back to the village cove.

They landed on the shingle. Not a soul was around. But, as they sat in the boat, Darra spotted a figure coming down towards them on the broken zigzag path that led from the headland.

'Cail!' she said, jumping ashore.

'Let's hide,' Bawn said. 'He'll make us drown ourselves all over again.'

'No – look, he's waving. He's already seen us.'

The figure drew near, and Cail seemed as never in life, a shadow half in this world, half in the Sidé. She could see his dark robe, but also beyond it to the rocks.

'Ah,' he said. 'You're back.'

They gaped at him, as at a ghost.

He produced a small sack. 'Here's some bread, water, fish. You've a long journey.'

He put the provisions in the boat.

'Cail,' Darra managed. 'Did the lightning strike you? Was it Dond's curse? Are you alive – or dead?'

'The storm did claim three lives,'

Cail said. 'Two villagers were lost this day.'

'Who?'

'Never mind; no friends of yours, anyway.'

Darra thought of the fat man who'd licked his chops and the thin neighbour with the pointed nose. 'Who was the third person killed – it wasn't you, was it?'

Cail smiled. 'It would take more than a lightning strike to finish me,' he said. 'The third was a certain foul-smelling witch in the mountains . . .'

'Olca!' Bawn exclaimed.

'Good riddance,' Darra said.

'But what about the curse?' Bawn asked. 'Will Dond come back and do worse damage if I stay alive?'

'No. His curse is broken.' Cail

pointed to the headland. They realized
something had changed. The standing
stone, a landmark for years, had
toppled to the ground.

'But how?' Darra gasped. 'Why?'

'You should know, Darra. Haven't I
had you reciting the ancient testaments
ever since you could talk? Not just what
the stone said – others too.'

Darra frowned. Then she
remembered. 'That funny little rhyme.
The one you sang to me when I was a
tiny tot in the bath –

Water, water, friend of Dond
Suck me down and spin me round
Till I reach the ocean bed
Where the sprites and fairies tread.
There my Mam will kiss and save me
And your wicked curse will leave me.'

Cail nodded. 'Your mother Meb –
by loving you both, in the end, enough
to die for you – ended Dond's curse. The
villagers are free of it. And as for Meb,
never fear for her. Lug loved her and she
is still with you, only in another form.'

'Oh,' Bawn gasped. 'Mam – she's
with us still?'

Cail nodded.

'Will I talk to her again? Will I see
her?'

Cail considered. 'Maybe,' he said.

'What about the villagers?' Darra
asked. 'Do they know they are free of
the curse?'

Cail smiled. 'They think that Dond
is appeased, but that Lug is angry – for
having killed you all. They're shivering
under their beds as we speak, too
frightened to come out. There'll be no

more drownings: not when they see what's happened to the standing stone.'

He motioned them both into the boat. 'Hurry now,' he said. 'Your time here in Inniscaul is over. The tide is turning. You must go.'

'Cail,' pleaded Darra, as she climbed aboard and he pushed them off again. 'Can't you come with us?'

'Row south,' Cail said, ignoring her question. 'Then east. You'll reach the mainland tomorrow.'

The boat surged as a wave cupped under it and dragged it out from the shingle.

'Cail!' Darra and Bawn shouted.

The old man smiled and shook his head. 'Away with you!' he called. 'The tide's with you, now!'

He waved goodbye, and they
watched the cove, the village, the keep,
the Inniscaul hills, the curves of the
island that had been their life drift away.
The figure of Cail grew smaller. Just as
Darra thought she could no longer make
him out, he turned into a bird and flew
off into a passing cloud.

'Did you see that?' Bawn gasped.

Darra nodded. 'Know what I think?

Cail, the blackbird, Lug – they're all
one.'

Bawn considered. 'But when the bird
landed on Mam's head,' he said, 'on the
beach, Cail was standing right beside
her. Don't you remember?'

'If Lug made us into two, where we
should've been one,' Darra murmured,
'maybe he can do the same to himself.'

Bawn rowed on, south then east
through a short summer night under
a waning moon. As he rowed, Darra
sang her bathtub song. The joys and

sadnesses of the world travelled with
them. Although they did not notice her,
a grey-whiskered seal with wise sunken
eyes swam alongside them. The next
day they reached a gleaming coast of
white sand. Reeds whistled a welcome
on the dunes. They disembarked,
newcomers to the land of Eriu, and
headed inland. A seal emerged from
the water and followed, turning into a
squirrel as she pattered across
the beach.

Author's note: Eriu *is an ancient
name for Eire, or Ireland.*

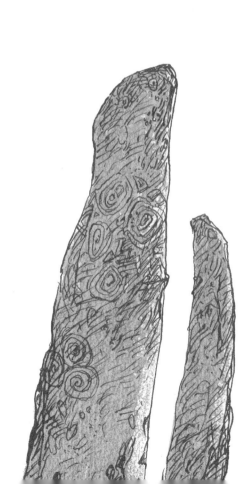

About Siobhan Dowd

Siobhan Dowd lived in Oxford with her husband, Geoff, before tragically dying from cancer in 2007, aged forty-seven. She was both an extraordinary writer and an extraordinary person.

Before her short career as an author, Siobhan directed the 'Freedom to Write' programme in New York and was named one of the 'Top 100 Irish-Americans' for her global anti-censorship work.

Returning to the UK, Siobhan worked for PEN International and co-founded a programme which takes authors into schools, prisons, young offender institutions and community projects.

Siobhan's first novel, *A Swift Pure Cry*, won the Branford Boase and the Eilis Dillon awards, and was shortlisted for the Carnegie Medal and Booktrust Teenage Prize.

Her second novel, *The London Eye Mystery*, won the NASEN & TES Special Educational Needs Children's Book Award. In the same year Siobhan was named as one of Waterstone's twenty-five British writers for the future.

Siobhan's third novel, *Bog Child*, was the first book to be posthumously awarded the Carnegie Medal.

A Monster Calls, a novel based on Siobhan's final idea, was written by Patrick Ness and illustrated by

Jim Kay, winning the Carnegie and Kate Greenway medals simultaneously in 2012.

In the very last days before she died, Siobhan set up The Siobhan Dowd Trust. It was the final act of someone who had spent so much of her life working on behalf of others. For further information, please see www.siobhandowdtrust.com.

About Pam Smy

Pam Smy studied Illustration at Anglia Ruskin University, going on to complete the MA in Children's Book Illustration in 2004. She has illustrated books by, among others, former Children's Laureate and author of *The Gruffalo*, Julia Donaldson, author Linda Newbery (for her award-winning novel *Lob*) and Sir Arthur Conan Doyle.

Pam is a lecturer on the world-renowned MA course in Children's Book Illustration at Anglia Ruskin University. She is a frequent exhibitor of her work as a printmaker, often as part of the Inky Crows artists' collective, of which she is a founder member. Pam lives in Cambridge.

THE RANSOM OF DOND
A DAVID FICKLING BOOK 978 0 857 56090 2

Published in Great Britain by David Fickling Books,
a division of Random House Children's Publishers UK
A Random House Group Company

This edition published 2013

1 3 5 7 9 10 8 6 4 2

DAVID FICKLING BOOKS
31 Beaumont Street, Oxford, OX1 2NP

www.kidsatrandomhouse.co.uk
www.totallyrandombooks.co.uk
www.randomhouse.co.uk

Addresses for companies within The Random House Group Limited
can be found at: www.randomhouse.co.uk/offices.htm

THE RANDOM HOUSE GROUP Limited Reg. No. 954009

A CIP catalogue record for this book is available from the British Library.

Printed and bound in Italy